TECH TRACK™

BUILDING YOUR CAREER IN IT

BECOMING A DATA ENGINEER

LAURA LA BELLA

Rosen YA™

New York

Published in 2018 by The Rosen Publishing Group, Inc.
29 East 21st Street, New York, NY 10010

First Edition

Library of Congress Cataloging-in-Publication Data

Names: La Bella, Laura, author.
Title: Becoming a data engineer / Laura La Bella.
Description: First edition. | New York City : Rosen Publishing, 2018. | Series: Tech track: building your career in IT | Includes bibliographical references and index.
Identifiers: LCCN 2016056441 | ISBN 9781508175506 (library bound)
Subjects: LCSH: Database design—Vocational guidance—Juvenile literature. | Database management—Vocational guidance—Juvenile literature. | Information technology—Vocational guidance—Juvenile literature.
Classification: LCC QA76.9.D26 L3 2018 | DDC 005.7—dc23
LC record available at https://lccn.loc.gov/2016056441

Manufactured in the United States of America

Contents

INTRODUCTION

App developer, web programmer, database administrator, security specialist, software developer...these are some of the more traditional job titles in the field of information technology. But as the world of computing continues to evolve, new career paths are emerging to address the growing needs of an industry that is constantly changing.

The computing industry is immersed in a big data revolution. Every day enormous amounts of information are collected. Sourced from nearly every interaction we have, from smartphones, social media accounts, and internet searches to retail purchases in stores and online, satellite information, banking transactions, and more, this information—as well as all of the efforts to gather, store, organize, and analyze it—is referred to as big data.

Big data has become a big deal because hidden within these massive collections of information are insights that reveal so much about so many things, from shopping behaviors and weather trends to predicting illnesses and tracking topics people are talking about. Within all of this big data are patterns, trends, and tendencies that can provide valuable amounts of information that help inform and influence companies, businesses, organizations, and the government. Big data has resulted in the need for a new set of professional skills to help organize, manage, and mine these massive reservoirs of information.

Big data sets are collected through a series of interconnected communication systems, including GPS satellites, internet searches, retail purchases, and more.

As a result of this constant stream of digital information, the demand for IT specialists to understand all aspects of this information—including collection, management, storage, organization, and analysis—is high. It has resulted in a new breed of computing professional whose job is to oversee these different aspects of big data.

A data engineer is a new type of IT professional who combines a number of computing skills to manage the enormous amounts of data being collected.

Among a variety of career paths that have emerged since the evolution of big data, data engineers are representative of a new wave of IT professionals. Data engineers are the designers, builders, and managers of the information, creating the infrastructure needed to store, process, and analyze information. The data engineer is an IT professional that makes sure big data infrastructure functions correctly on a day-to-day basis. Data engineers develop the architecture—the set of rules and methods that describe the functionality, organization, and operation of a computer system—that organizes, analyzes, and supplies this data in the way their employers require it. They also make sure that these complex computing systems are performing smoothly. Data engineers work as one piece on a team of IT professionals that all serve to manage the big data puzzle.

Many computing experts have already predicted a shortage of skilled workers to fill these data engineering positions. With demand this high,

As big data grows and its uses become more significant, data engineers will play an increasingly critical role in the success of how this information is stored, used, and mined.

jobs will be available in all types of industries that seek to use big data to help better understand their businesses, their customers, and others. It's an exciting career field that will continue to grow and evolve as the big data revolution continues to advance.

CHAPTER ONE

IT: A Young, Dynamic Industry

Computing touches nearly every aspect of our modern lives. It assists us in accomplishing a wide range of everyday tasks, from the mundane (checking email, launching a smartphone app, or recording a TV show on our DVR) to the complex (diagnosing diseases, encrypting sensitive financial information, and enabling Google Maps to provide driving directions based on location). Information technology (IT) is often used to describe all aspects of computing. It's what makes all things possible when you use any type of computer or computing device, like a laptop, smartphone, or tablet.

What Is IT?

IT is the study, design, development, implementation, and use of computers and computing systems, such as hardware and software, storage systems, networking,

Computers are all around us. They operate our coffee makers and cars, enable us to stay connected, and allow us to learn more at the touch of our fingers.

and other physical devices to collect, process, and distribute all different forms of electronic information. IT has become an essential function in nearly all aspects of daily modern life. Every single business, company, organization, and government agency uses IT, whether it is to manage manufacturing, access health records, maintain employee files, track financial transactions, run social media campaigns, engage in customer relations, communicate with consumers, share news, or otherwise. And every day, nearly every person uses a device or product such as a phone, television, or MP3 player that is powered by IT.

IT and Big Data

Collecting information and data is not a new idea. In fact, since humans began recording history, many different types of information have been collected and shared—first through oral tradition and then, as written language developed, using tools to transcribe information by hand and through printed means. Societies around the world documented and tracked weather trends, historical events, important scientific developments, and more.

With the advent of computers, collecting and storing data became even easier. Today data is collected and stored on servers created, monitored, and maintained by IT professionals. This data is vast and covers all facets of

Collecting information is one of the oldest methods of recording history. Ancient Egyptian hieroglyphics are one of the first forms of data collection used for people and events.

our lives. Long-term data can predict trends for rainfall and temperature that have helped farmers decide when to plant crops. Land records show precise property lines for homeowners. Phone books reveal where people live and how to contact them.

A new type of data emerged when the internet launched and web pages became a destination for all kinds of information. Companies began collecting data on what news stories were being read, where people were shopping, what they were searching for on websites, the types of music being downloaded, the kinds of videos being watched, the number of people visiting a particular web site, and more. When social media sites such as Facebook, Twitter, Instagram, and LinkedIn were introduced, people began to volunteer all kinds of personal information about themselves, such as the birth of children, where they ate on Friday night, trips to the emergency room, political affiliations, places they vacationed, job promotions and employment moves, commentary on current events, movies watched, concerts attended—the list goes on. All of this data was, and is, constantly collected. Pair all of this personal information with data collected from smartphones, sensors on traffic signals, point-of-sale terminals at retail stores and through online shopping, consumer products such as fitness trackers, graphics, weblogs, electronic health records, market research focus groups, and customer ratings of restaurants, and you start to get an idea of the tremendous amount of data that is collected, stored, and analyzed on a daily basis. This is all big data.

You may not realize that you're already familiar with the concept of big data and some of the ways it can be used. On websites like Amazon and Netflix, recommendations are made to you based on your interests. Using complex algorithms and analysis of your previous purchases and your search history, Amazon and Netflix can make educated predictions about your likes and dislikes to recommend movies, books, and television shows you are likely to be interested in watching or purchasing.

Today, we wear technology that collects information about us. Apps like fitness trackers on our smartwatches monitor our steps using GPS and share our data with others.

Why Is Big Data a Big Deal?

John R. Mashey, a chief scientist for SGI, a company known for high performance computing, coined the term "big data" in the late 1990s to describe how the boundaries of computing keep growing. As data was being collected and stored, many businesses and organizations began to understand that if they analyzed all of this data they could get significant value from what the information was able to tell them.

One of the reasons why big data is so important is that hidden within these massive collections of information are valuable insights that can tell us so much about so many things. The computing world saw big data's potential in 2008 when Google was able to predict the outbreak of the flu in seven regions of the United States. Every day, Google processes billions and billions of searches and collects data on all of the topics users are exploring. The company decided to track and analyze searches for terms such as "flu symptoms," "cough," "fever," and "aches and pains." Google knows what states its users live in, and based on the search terms and geography, the company was able to predict flu outbreaks two weeks faster than the Centers for Disease Control and Prevention (CDC).

The CDC tracks the flu by using what they call "traditional flu surveillance systems," which includes a variety of data, such as lab results from patients that have flulike symptoms, information provided by doctors about patient visits, and observa-

While analyzing the web searches of flu symptoms by Google users, analysts realized the immense potential of big data and how it could be used.

tion of admitted flu patients at hospitals. This data can take up to two weeks to collect and analyze. Google's search queries are immediate and can be analyzed quickly to detect a pattern.

This is just one example of the power of collecting information and analyzing it for patterns to produce information that's both valuable and useful.

Quality Is More Important Than Quantity

Organizations that began to use big data quickly learned

that big data was less about the amount of information being collected and more about the quality of the data and what they could do with it. Many leading computer scientists believe that the big data revolution taking place right now is more about the computational power that exists to analyze, understand, and apply information gleaned from big data than the act of collecting data and storing it.

Big data is collected and analyzed for nearly all industries, including government, manufacturing, health care, education, media, and science. Some of the ways the analysis of big data can inform an organization include:

» In manufacturing data can influence costs, productivity, and innovation.
» In health care data can improve personalized medicine, prescriptive analytics, clinical risk intervention, and predictive analytics.
» In science and research data can be read and analyzed significantly faster for interpretation, and research results and patterns can be better filtered.
» In retail data can predict sales volume, buying trends, and consumer behavior.

The benefits of big data are significant. Using big data can provide an organization with timely information about products and services and can influence their improvement; organizations can respond quicker to scenarios revealed by the analysis of big data.

In-store and online purchases can tell a company about buying behavior and consumer preferences. They also show patterns that indicate wealth, family dynamics, and more.

Emerging Career Fields

Big data applies to nearly all industries, and as a result, every type of organization is hiring data-related positions. As more and more data is collected every single day, the need for IT professionals with experience and knowledge of big data, its current and potential uses, and its future applications will only continue to grow. The demand for information management specialists who can help manage the collection, storage, organization, and analysis of this massive amount of information is high. As a result,

Types of Big Data

It can be overwhelming to think about the vast amounts of big data being collected each day. Big data can be split into two categories, "structured" and "unstructured," and within those categories, further grouping helps define the types of information being gathered.

Structured data is information that already exists in an organized manner, such as on spreadsheets or in databases. It's already searchable. Examples of structured data include:

Created data: Information put together by a business from areas such as consumer survey and focus group results, consumer information gathered at point-of-sale modules, shopping trends and behavior collected using customer loyalty cards, and behavior exhibited during online shopping.

Provoked data: Opportunities for customers to give their opinions. This can include product and restaurant reviews.

Transaction data: Information collected at the time of purchase, such as behavior leading up to the transaction and clicks on banner advertising.

Compiled data: Information such as demographics, magazine subscriptions, and automobile registrations.

Experimental data: Results from a business experimenting with various marketing campaigns or advertising placements to learn what messages may be most effective.

Unstructured data is information that is not organized neatly in existing databases and resembles things like websites clicks and social media posts. Examples of unstructured data include:

Captured data: Collecting information such as internet searches.

User-generated data: Content created by an individual, including tweets and retweets, posts to social media accounts, and videos posted and/or viewed online.

new career fields have emerged where IT professionals with specific sets of skills are in demand to help organizations manage all of this data. One of these careers is data engineer.

A data engineer builds the massive reservoirs that hold big data. They develop, construct, test, and maintain architectures such as databases and large-scale data processing systems that house big data. Data engineers must be able to build systems that can accommodate the three Vs of big data: "volume," which refers to the vast amount of data being collected; "velocity," or the speed at which data is collected; and "variety," or the wide range of types of data collected. Once data engineers put these processing systems in place, these huge pools of information are ready for other IT professionals, who are skilled in pulling the information they need to analyze it for trends and patterns. But first, that data must be contained and housed in a system that works for each individual organization's data.

CHAPTER TWO

WHAT IS A DATA ENGINEER?

Data engineers, along with the wealth of new career paths that have emerged since the evolution of big data, are a new breed of IT professional. Data engineers are the designers, builders, and managers of the information, or the big data infrastructure. In this context, the term "infrastructure" refers to the tools needed to store, process, and analyze information. Those tools can be a mix of hardware such as servers, which are devices used primarily for storing information, and software, which are programs and operating instructions for your computer. Data engineers build the systems that store data, making sure it is stored securely, can flow smoothly from its source to its destination, and is accessible for the IT professionals who need to analyze the data for valuable insights.

Working on teams that include other IT professionals who specialize in big data (such as data scientists, data analysts, and data architects), data

The information collected as big data is stored on hundreds of thousands of servers located around the world.

engineers ensure the data is held in a working, sustainable system.

What Does a Data Engineer Do?

The career path of a data engineer may be new, but it combines existing technologies to manage data and the databases that hold this information. Each of the tasks expected of a data engineer is different and may require a combination of educational and experiential knowledge and skills. You may be expected to do all of them if your organization is small, a few of them if it's a mid-size company, or you may specialize in just one area if you're employed by a large corporation.

A data engineer is responsible for a number of key duties. These activities may include:

» Designing, constructing, installing, testing, and maintaining data management systems and infrastructures
» Understanding the needs of an organization and matching them to the right kind of computing and database system
» Ensuring that database systems continue to meet an organization's changing needs
» Maintaining the safety and security of a computing system to protect data from cyber threats, such as hacking
» Researching ways to gather and use information
» Developing processes for searching large databases and producing the information needed
» Integrating new data management tools, as they become available, into existing systems to improve storage, security, or other aspects of data management
» Creating custom software and/or applications to help produce more exact information based on the data requested
» Acquiring extensive knowledge of a wide variety of programming languages and computing tools

and combining them to create more effective database systems

- Installing and updating recovery procedures for the loss of data
- Recommending ways to improve data reliability, increase efficiency of data mining, and maintain data quality
- Collaborating with a big data team of additional computing professionals

Managing big data is a team effort requiring computing professionals, including data engineers, network administrators, computing security specialists, and web programmers.

The Difference Between a Data Engineer, a Data Analyst, and a Data Scientist

With all of the new job titles resulting from the evolution and growth of big data—data engineer, data analyst, data scientist—it can be difficult to determine what each role does and how they differ from one another when their titles all sound so similar. But each job has its own place and a distinct set of responsibilities on a big data team.

The Data Engineer: A data engineer prepares the infrastructure that holds the data and helps to create ways to organize the data so that when a query is designed, the information can be accessed and produced efficiently.

The Data Analyst: A data analyst is the person that helps an organization define what they are looking for and creates the query, or the request, needed to extract the correct data from a database. In other words, if a company wants to know what products sold well on Black Friday, the biggest holiday shopping day of the year, the data analyst will create the query that produces the information needed from the database to answer that question. They provide the data, however they do not analyze it, despite the job's title. Nor do they have a mathematical or statistical background needed to interpret the data to discover trends or patterns.

The Data Scientist: A data scientist is the IT professional who turns raw data into information that is understandable.

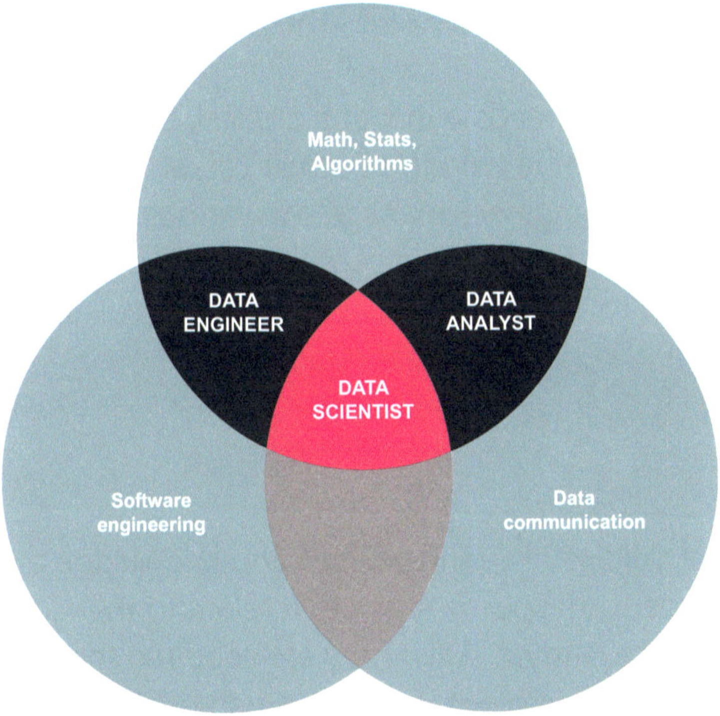

Using a combination of statistics and analytics, a data scientist helps an organization take the immense amount of data it has collected and turn it into information that shows patterns, trends, or insights that a company can use to make decisions. Data scientists have strong programming and math skills that assist them in creating processes for searching big data, analytical skills for examining and evaluating data, and communication skills for interpreting and presenting their findings.

All three of these jobs rely on the others to create a big data system that works well, functions effectively, and produces the information an organization needs.

A Combination of Skills

A data engineer needs a mix of technical, business, and personal skills to be effective in their career. Each set of skills helps the data engineer manage the various roles they have, whether they are managing complex databases, presenting information to organizational leadership, or collaborating on a team of other IT professionals.

Technical Skills

Technical skills refer to the abilities and knowledge a person needs to perform specific tasks that relate to their job. Technical skills are learned skills. They are acquired through high school and college courses, or by self-study. For a data engineer, these skills include expertise and knowledge in:

Hadoop-based technologies: Hadoop is a collection of different products (MapReduce, HIVE, HDFS, YARN, and Spark) that all have different uses, but work together to process and analyze data quickly. Hadoop is open source, which refers to software where its original coding is made available to anyone to use or to modify based on their needs. The main idea of Hadoop is that it allows the user to break up sections of data to process and analyze them all at the same time, instead of processing an entire mass of data at once. By breaking the data up, the information can be processed and analyzed faster.

SQL-based technologies: Short for Structured Query Language, SQL-based programming languages (such as PostgreSQL and MySQL) are used to manage information in a database management system, from adding, updating and deleting rows of data to retrieving sets of information from a database for an IT professional to later analyze.

Data modeling tools: Data modeling is the creation of a document that diagrams a software system using text and symbols that explains the way data needs to flow. It details the relationships between data. Examples of data modeling tools include ERStudio, DBWrench, and TOAD Data Modeler.

Programming languages: Computers need to be told what to do. Programming languages are those instructions. Some popular programming languages include Python, C++, dBASE, XML, and Perl.

Data analysis software: This software cuts through data to find patterns, trends or relationships between information. This software is essential in helping to mine or search the data. DataMelt, KNIME, Orange, JMatLab, and SAS are among hundreds of data analysis software available.

Data warehousing solutions: A data warehouse is a central place where data is collected. Multiple places may send data to a data warehouse. Data engineers need to know how to manage these systems, accounting for size and knowing when to increase it.

Operating systems: An operating system manages all of the other programs and software loaded onto a computer. Most computers come with an initial operating system. You can also install different operating systems depending on the tasks you need your computer to manage. Some common operating systems are UNIX, Linux, Solaris, and MS Windows.

BUSINESS SKILLS

Business skills refer to your ability to interact with others properly while achieving goals for your organization. These skills include:

Creative problem solving: Things don't always go the way you expect them to, and you'll be expected to not only adapt to the unexpected, but to help solve problems efficiently and effectively.

Critical thinking: This valuable skill helps you to see things from different points of view. When you ask questions and seek out information from many different viewpoints, you are broadening your knowledge and perspective.

Discipline, time management, and focus: In our digital age of social media and information overload, it can be easy to check your email, scroll through Facebook, and waste half of your day. Managing distractions is vital to getting work done; so is time management, which refers to planning and controlling the amount of time spent on a particular activity or task.

Effective collaboration: More than ever people are being asked to work on teams of people from all areas of an organization. Working together, communicating ideas, and listening to others is important. Carefully listen to management, data scientists, and data architects to establish their needs.

Curiosity: This is an active state of interest where you continually want to know more. People who are curious tend to learn faster, have deeper relationships with others, and are interested in broadening their knowledge on all sorts of topics. In business, it can lead to effective change and better collaboration on teams.

Communication skills: The ability to share your ideas with others, make an argument for a cause, write clear and concise proposals, and interact effectively with others are all communication skills.

Industry knowledge: Better understanding of how your industry works is essential to creating solutions to specific problems. Knowing the types of information a health care professional might need from a database is vastly different from what a manufacturing company might need. As a data engineer, your knowledge of your industry will inform how you might choose to organize information in a database.

Communication is key for computing. Data engineers and other IT professionals working with big data must present information and make decisions as part of a group.

PERSONAL SKILLS

Personal skills are work-related abilities people have that are based on individual traits rather than learned skills (such as knowing a programing language). Accountability, reliability, loyalty, leadership, friendliness, patience, thoughtfulness, creativity, resourcefulness, attention to detail, and dependability are all considered personal skills.

Most people naturally possess personal skills, though you can further develop them. By completing tasks on time, you are working on becoming more dependable. Taking on supervisory tasks can help you develop leadership skills as you learn to guide others in their day-to-day work. Keeping a level head and being patient during stressful times, particularly while others may be acting on impulse, will help you make decisions in a calmer frame of mind. These skills can make a big difference in your career and help position you for further advancement as your technical and business skills grow.

CHAPTER THREE

THE KNOWLEDGE YOU NEED

A career as a data engineer can be an exciting profession, filled with opportunities to contribute to and guide the vision for an organization's data infrastructure and business tools, and to work with a team of IT professionals in an emerging, dynamic field of study.

The educational background needed to become a data engineer combines computer science, computer engineering, information technology, mathematics, and programming with mathematics and scientific analysis. These subject areas aren't new, but they involve a variety of skills you must learn to combine and master in order to become an effective data engineer.

To be considered for a career as a data engineer requires a bachelor's degree, which is a four year course of study at the college level that combines specific course work in computing, programming, information technology, and software engineering with liberal arts courses in subjects such as English, history, and the social sciences. Preparation for a job as a data engineer can begin as early as high school, where you can begin to develop key skills you'll need later.

Math skills are a key requirement for IT professionals. Taking advanced math classes in high school can help prepare you for an IT program in college.

HIGH SCHOOL: LAYING A STRONG FOUNDATION IN COMPUTING

For many students, an interest in a particular career path begins in high school, when students are beginning to think about their aptitude and interest in various subjects. This is often a time when students decide they like a particular subject area, such as computer programming or history, and are interested in learning what career opportunities exist in those fields.

For students interested in computing and IT, many schools offer regular courses and special activities in topics such as computing and programming to help you build a foundation of knowledge in computer science. For high school students interested in careers in computing, courses in mathematics (algebra, precalculus, calculus, trigonometry, and geometry) and computer science (programming, programming languages, information assurance, and cyber security) will help you build initial knowledge of the field and assist in establishing a strong foundation of skills that you'll develop further in college.

Many high schools also offer clubs that focus on computing, technology, and engineering. These activities can boost a student's interest in a particular subject area and expose them to new ideas through projects and team-based events. Project Lead The Way is an educational organization that runs programs in the sciences, computing, and engineering in more than nine thousand schools throughout the United States. According to the organization's website, Project Lead The Way's computer science program "not only builds knowledge and skills in computer science, but also empowers students to develop essential skills such as problem solving, critical and creative thinking, communication, collaboration, and perseverance." Organizations such as Project Lead The Way help students build their computer science skills as they learn more about the wide range of computing jobs. These programs also pair students with professionals working in their local communities. These computing professionals serve as mentors and help illustrate what it's like to work for a real computing company.

Programs designed for high school students that are offered by colleges can help you gain knowledge in areas of computing and mathematics, further preparing you for success in college.

Several colleges and universities such as Stanford, Florida Institute of Technology, and the University of Texas offer summer programs in computing. In these programs, students attend immersive programs where they study a particular area of computing such as computer science, mathematics, or programming. Students are taught by each institution's faculty; in some cases, students live on campus to get a taste of college life. Students get to discover something new about the field, gain new skills, and further prepare themselves for academic programs at the college level.

In addition to college programs for high school students, several organizations also offer camps for students interested in the computing field. Pathways to Science and iD Tech Camps both offer summer experiences for high school students in computing, IT, mathematics, and programming.

College-Level Course Work

Many data engineers choose to earn a bachelor's of science degree in computer science, software engineering, applied mathematics, statistics, or a related field. Because of the highly technical nature of the career, a college degree is a necessity. Each of these majors shares course work in basic computing, programming, and math, but each offers a slightly different level of advanced knowledge.

Computer science programs typically attract mathematically adept students. Course work in this major is heavy on math and includes calculus, discrete mathematics, probability and statistics, and linear algebra. Computing courses usually include computer systems, programming, computer science theory, and computer architecture.

Software engineering programs focus on artificial intelligence, business applications, computational mathematics, computer security, statistics, and usability. Programs tend to connect software engineering principles to application areas, such as health care, finance, engineering, or economics. Students study courses in

College programs offer a wide range of courses that will teach you the foundations of computing, along with specialty areas such as computing security and networking.

models of software, software subsystems, computer systems, software process and project management, computer programming, human-computer interaction, and software design.

Applied mathematics is a combination of mathematics with specialized knowledge of a particular field, such as engineering, computing, or technology. This course of study is heavy on math with elective courses in an area of study where a student wants to apply those math skills, such as big data.

A career as a data engineer can begin with any of these majors, as all of them will help you develop the skills you need to be successful in the field. Choosing one particular area might depend more on the subtopic of data engineering you like the most. If you wish to write programming code, computer science might be the best option for you. If you like designing software, software engineering would be a strong choice. If you prefer the mathematical side of data engineering, applied mathematics or statistics would be a great fit for you.

OTHER EDUCATIONAL OPTIONS

While a bachelor's degree is essential for entry into the field, vocational or technical programs might offer you either a strong foundation to build upon or an opportunity for you to add additional skills if your educational background is in an area unrelated to computing.

Vocational programs are shorter courses of study. They include courses that directly relate to preparing a student for entry into a career. Unlike bachelor's degree programs, where your course work includes liberal arts (like history and English) and sciences courses, vocational programs offer introductory courses in a specific area of study, such as computing or engineering. Students who complete vocational programs tend to work in support of professionals in these areas. Vocational programs can be a more cost effective way to gain knowledge or a chance to change career fields.

Several certificate programs have emerged that address various areas of big data. These programs, which are often three or five courses in length, are offered to professionals who want to gain knowledge in the dynamic and evolving big data field. They are usually college courses at either the undergraduate or graduate levels. They can provide a foundation for a computing professional who has a background in a different area, offer knowledge for the computing professional who is interested in changing their career, or they may be added onto an existing program to broaden a student's knowledge.

There is one certification program in particular that is known as a solid, all-around credential for general database professionals. The Certified Data Management Professional (CDMP) certification program was developed by DAMA International, a database management association, for computing professionals who work with databases. It is well recognized by IT professionals and can add to your level of expertise and knowledge of databases and big data.

The CDMP is offered at four levels—associate, practitioner, master, or fellow—and awarded to candidates who provide evidence of education and experience and who pass the CDMP's professional knowledge exam. Each level includes minimum requirements for experience, with associates requiring the least (less than two years) and fellows requiring the most (more than twenty years). Each level also has its own baseline for educational requirements, professional experience (including managing and leading others in the field), and contributions to the database field, which can include being an active member of

Top Fifteen Colleges for the Study of Computer Science, Computing, and Information Technology

Each year, *US News & World Report* ranks the best colleges and universities in most academic disciplines. The magazine has ranked the following colleges and universities as among the best in the world to study computer science:

1. Massachusetts Institute of Technology, Cambridge, MA (web.mit.edu)
2. Stanford University, Stanford, CA (www.stanford.edu)
3. Harvard University, Cambridge, MA (www.harvard.edu)
4. University of California-Berkeley, Berkeley, CA (www.berkeley.edu)
5. Tsinghua University, Beijing, China (www.tsinghua.edu)
6. University of Texas-Austin, Austin, TX (www.utexas.edu)
7. Nanyang Technological University, Singapore (www.ntu.edu.sg)
8. Princeton University, Princeton, NJ (www.princeton.edu)
9. University of California-San Diego, San Diego, CA (www.ucsd.edu)
10. National University of Singapore, Singapore (www.nus.edu.sg)

11. University of California–Los Angeles, Los Angeles, CA (www.ucla.edu)
12. Georgia Institute of Technology, Atlanta, GA (www.gatech.edu)
13. Hong Kong University of Science and Technology, Hong Kong (www.ust.hk)
14. Carnegie Mellon University, Pittsburgh, PA (www.cmu.edu)
15. University of Southern California, Los Angeles, CA (www.usc.edu)

a local ICCP chapter, presenting at conferences, teaching workshops, or writing and publishing papers.

WILL I NEED A MASTER'S DEGREE?

A master's degree is an advanced degree of study that follows the completion of a bachelor's degree. Master's degrees are often one to two years in length and are highly focused on a particular topic, giving you expertise in a specific area of study. A master's degree in a computing-related area, such as information technology, big data science, computer science, or an area of mathematics such as applied mathematics or statistics, is not needed for entry into the big data field, nor is it a requirement for a career as a data engineer. Many computing professionals become more specialized in an aspect of data engineering once they begin their job.

Advanced course work offered through master's degree programs can further hone your skills and give you expert- level knowledge of the field.

A master's degree may be more helpful to the IT professional who has a desire to advance in a leadership role at their organization. A master's degree in information technology, business, management, or finance can provide an overview of management skills that could be useful as a computing professional is promoted to a supervisory role that oversees other computing professionals.

CHAPTER FOUR

INTERNSHIPS AND CO-OPS

When you are ready to start applying for jobs as a data engineer, how can you ensure that your résumé will stand out from the crowd? Complete an internship or cooperative education experience to gain the on-the-job knowledge you need to be competitive in the job market.

Internships and cooperative education, or co-ops, are the most important ways to gain on-the-job experience in your chosen career field. College students who have an internship or co-op listed on their résumés are more likely to get job offers after graduation versus students who choose not to pursue these experiences.

Internships and co-ops are valuable experiences for students. They provide a clear look at the day-to-day workings of a career field, allow students to apply the knowledge they have gained in the classroom to a real-world setting, help narrow a student's career aspirations, help connect students to professionals in the field, and give students a chance to work on real projects where they can actively contribute to their career field.

What Is an Internship/Co-op?

An internship or co-op provides job training. Students apply to internship and co-op positions much like they would a real job. Many internships and co-ops in the computing field are paid, which enables a student to earn money while they are learning on the job.

Internships and co-ops can vary in length, depending on the company and each individual opportunity. Some may last for a summer, while others may be the length of a college semester (twelve to sixteen weeks). Some colleges offer internship and co-operative education programs where students are allowed to alternate periods of study on campus with arranged periods of time away from campus for an internship or co-operative education placement. In some of these programs, students may extend their degree to five years, instead of the traditional four years, to accommodate the time they spend interning or on co-op.

Once hired by an organization, interns and co-ops are assigned to a supervisor, who oversees their work. The supervisor is often a professional in their field of study who assigns projects and tasks, provides any training the student needs, and evaluates their performance. They may also serve as a mentor, offering career advice and guidance.

Benefits of an Internship or Co-op

Students and employers both benefit from the internship/co-op experience. For interns and co-ops, working in your desired career field gives you the opportunity to gain insights you can only get on the job. While your college course work will give you the theoretical understanding of the skills and knowledge required of your career field, being able to apply that knowledge on a day-to-day basis

Internships vs. Co-ops: What's the Difference?

Many people think the words "internship" and "co-op" are interchangeable. While they are similar in that students get real-world, on-the-job experience, there is a difference between the two.

Internships are considered shorter stints of work, usually a few weeks to a month in length. Some internships are not paid, so a student must balance an internship with employment in order to support their college educational expenses.

While on a co-op or engaged in an internship, you'll meet professionals who can help guide your career as you learn from them on a daily basis.

A co-op is a longer period of work, typically an academic semester or quarter, or the length of a summer. Because you spend a longer stretch of time on a co-op, employers tend to give co-op students more meaningful work projects, or assignments that take longer to complete or are more comprehensive in nature. Students have more time to examine an issue, propose a solution, and implement a resolution. This maximizes a student's effort and provides a more thorough work experience.

is different. Internships and co-ops can help you make the transition from classroom learning to the hands-on, practical application of your education.

While interning or on co-op you will learn the inner workings of a company, what a computing professional does each day, and how your classroom knowledge applies on the job. You also get to work on real-world projects, where you can make a contribution using your knowledge and skills. For employers, interns and co-ops often serve as additional staff that can help an organization tackle projects to which they might not otherwise have been able to dedicate time or employees. They also get a firsthand look at potential employees. Many organizations hire the students who were former interns and co-ops. Whether the internship or co-op is paid or not, the benefits are well worth the time on the job.

An internship or co-op helps you show your skills to potential employers, who may be looking to hire you when you graduate.

Valuable work experience: Classroom learning, along with the assignments and projects assigned by professors, often teach the skills and theories of a career field. On-the-job training through an internship or co-op gives you the opportunity to apply those skills to real projects. You'll learn far more by applying your skills to solve a problem that has real-world consequences than a project that just illustrates a theory. Internships and co-ops give you the hands-on work experience you can't get in the classroom.

Build your and gain an edge on the job market: When you apply for your first job out of college, an organization wants to see more than just your grades and college activities listed on your résumé. An internship or co-op is real work experience that you can list on your résumé. It shows that you are familiar with the industry, have some entry-level experience, and gained some experience working on industry-related problems. In a competitive job market, where there are more applicants than jobs available, an internship or co-op can set you apart from the crowd of other people looking for a job.

Prove your skills: Organizations will often use their internship and co-op programs as a way to scout for new talent. A company gets to test you out as an intern or co-op to see if you can do the job and if you have the skills, aptitude, and personality that work well with their company culture and performance standards. Organizations like to see what type of employee you'll be, if you work hard, take initiative, seek out ways to improve, and look for opportunities to do more and expand your internship/co-op experience. Many companies offer their interns and co-ops full-time positions upon completion of the student's degree program.

Confirm your career path: An internship or co-op is not only a great way to gain experience in your career field, it's also the best way for you to learn the day-to-day operations of your job. And you might find out that it's not what you expected. You may discover that the long hours of looking at programming code is not as thrilling as you initially thought, or that the excitement of getting software to pull the data you need isn't as rewarding as you imagined. The only true way to learn what a career is like is if you spend time on the job. The good news is that since internships and co-ops are relatively short, one summer or one semester in length, you aren't making the commitment that a full-time job offer entails. You can complete the duration of your co-op and change course toward a field you find better suited to your interests.

Network: Networking, or meeting and staying in touch with professionals in your field, is key to learning about open job positions in your field and to building a professional network of people with more career experience than you have. Internships and co-ops are great ways to meet the leaders in your field. These professionals can provide guidance on career opportunities, alert you to openings in the field, provide advice on issues or problems you may face in the workforce, and support you through mentoring.

Boost your confidence and maturity: The more experience you gain during internships and co-ops, the more confidence you'll have as you apply for jobs. When you're on an interview, you'll have real world contributions to talk about when a hiring manager asks you to speak about a challenge you faced or a problem you needed to solve. You'll also feel more confident when you begin to apply for jobs, because you'll know that you can handle the demands of a position.

MAKE THE MOST OF YOUR INTERNSHIP OR CO-OP

Your internship or co-op will cover a relatively short duration of time—at most, the length of a summer or a semester of college—and it'll go by fast. In addition to learning skills and making contributions to the projects you are assigned to, you also need to make the most of your time in other ways:

Take advantage of opportunities: Does the organization need a task to be completed? Don't wait to be asked, volunteer to do it. It'll show you are interested in learning about other aspects of the company and it shows initiative.

Meet as many people as possible: You never know who might get promoted, who might leave the organization for an opportunity elsewhere, or who might become a helpful mentor for you down the road. By getting to know as many people as you can, you'll learn how the job you're doing connects with others at the company and contributes on a larger scale, and you'll make connections that could last throughout your professional career.

Attend professional events: Professional events, such as seminars and conferences, are a way for people in the career field to meet up with one another, talk about the issues they all face, and work together toward finding solutions to common problems. They are also ways to inform the industry of changes and provide education and professional development.

Work on a variety of projects: Don't just work on the project you are assigned; seek out opportunities to con-

Networking with professionals in your field can be invaluable. You'll have mentors to learn from, and you can gain a professional perspective on your career path.

tribute to other projects so you can learn more about the inner workings of the organization. Just remember that you were hired for a particular position, so be sure you have your supervisor's permission to take on more work. You want to be sure you're doing the job you were hired for and you're doing it well. If you cannot take on more work, or the project you are assigned to does not allow you to spend time working on other projects, you may want to seek out an opportunity to shadow another supervisor for a day or afternoon. This will give you insight into how another department functions and you may witness another style of leadership.

Ask for feedback on your performance: Don't wait until the end of your internship or co-op to find out how you are doing. After the first few weeks, ask for an informal review with your supervisor so you can gain feedback on the things you are doing well and the things that need work. That way, if some part of your job performance needs work, you have time to fix it and show you can improve and follow constructive criticism.

Make the most of constructive criticism: Your supervisor will provide you with feedback on things you could do better or ways you can improve. These comments should be provided in a friendly and supportive manner, and not in a critical, negative way. Constructive criticism is designed to help you learn where you can improve. It's not meant to hurt your feelings or be critical of your abilities. Learn from this feedback and look for opportunities to grow.

Ask questions: We learn by seeking out information. So ask questions to understand how your role benefits the company, how each division works together, and how your company influences the industry. Seek out information on the different people you work with and how they came to the jobs they are in. The more you know, the better you can make decisions for yourself and the more you gain by understanding the organization you are working for and the industry you are in.

CHAPTER FIVE

GETTING YOUR FIRST JOB

Careers in big data are in demand. The McKinsey Global Institute has predicted that by 2018 the US could face a shortage of between 140,000 to 190,000 professionals with the deep analytical skills needed to organize and understand big data. That means there will be plenty of jobs for people who have the computing skills to organize, manage, and store big data. The good news is that nearly every type of industry has a need for a big data engineer, including tech companies, health care organizations, educational institutions, private companies and corporations, and not-for-profits. There will be many opportunities for you to enter the field and to begin building your IT career.

Big data is an in-demand field and IT professionals with the right combination of skills are needed. This means a lot of opportunity for you!

HOW TO GET A JOB AS A DATA ENGINEER

The first thing you need to do when searching for a job as a data engineer is find out where job opportunities are listed. The best place to look for a job in computing is on the internet.

Job posting sites: A number of employment web sites have emerged as popular search sites for positions in the computing industry, among them: Dice.com, Jobpile.com, Petri.com, Authenticjobs.com, Simplyhired.com, Indeed.com, and Mosthired.com. These sites offer job postings, job boards, articles about various industries and job search advice. Some even advertise freelance work. Some of these sites—Dice.com, for example—specialize in computing fields.

Company web sites: Searching company web sites is also a useful task when looking for a job. Many companies post open positions on their companies websites. This also gives you an opportunity to learn more about specific companies

Job searches have become easier thanks to job posting websites, which link you to a lot of different jobs and opportunities in your area.

at the same time that you're seeking an open position. You might find that working as a data engineer is less stressful at a retail company than at a tech giant like Google. Or, you may discover that working for a leading computing company specializing in finance allows you to explore your personal interest in the financial industry while applying your big data skills.

Apply to a Job

Once you find an open position, applying is the next step in the process. The first thing you need is a résumé.

A résumé is a one- to two-page summary of your experience. It should be well-organized and broken down into sections that outline your career objectives, education, professional work experience, accomplishments, and any other applicable skills you have to offer. You should have a basic résumé ready so that once you begin searching for a job you can tailor it to meet the qualifications of an open job posting. If a job description details a specific skill you have, make sure it's listed—or better yet, if you have an accomplishment related to that skill, make sure it's on your résumé. You want your résumé to focus on the employer's needs, not just your own.

Your résumé highlights your skills, abilities, and accomplishments. It should look professional and be concise and tailored to each job application.

Ten Cities That Are Tech Hubs

Big data is happening everywhere, but these ten American cities stand out as hubs for computing professionals pursuing jobs in big data:

1. New York, NY
2. San Francisco, CA
3. Atlanta, GA
4. Seattle, WA
5. Chicago, IL
6. Austin, TX
7. Washington, DC
8. Boston, MA
9. Charlotte, NC
10. Dallas, TX

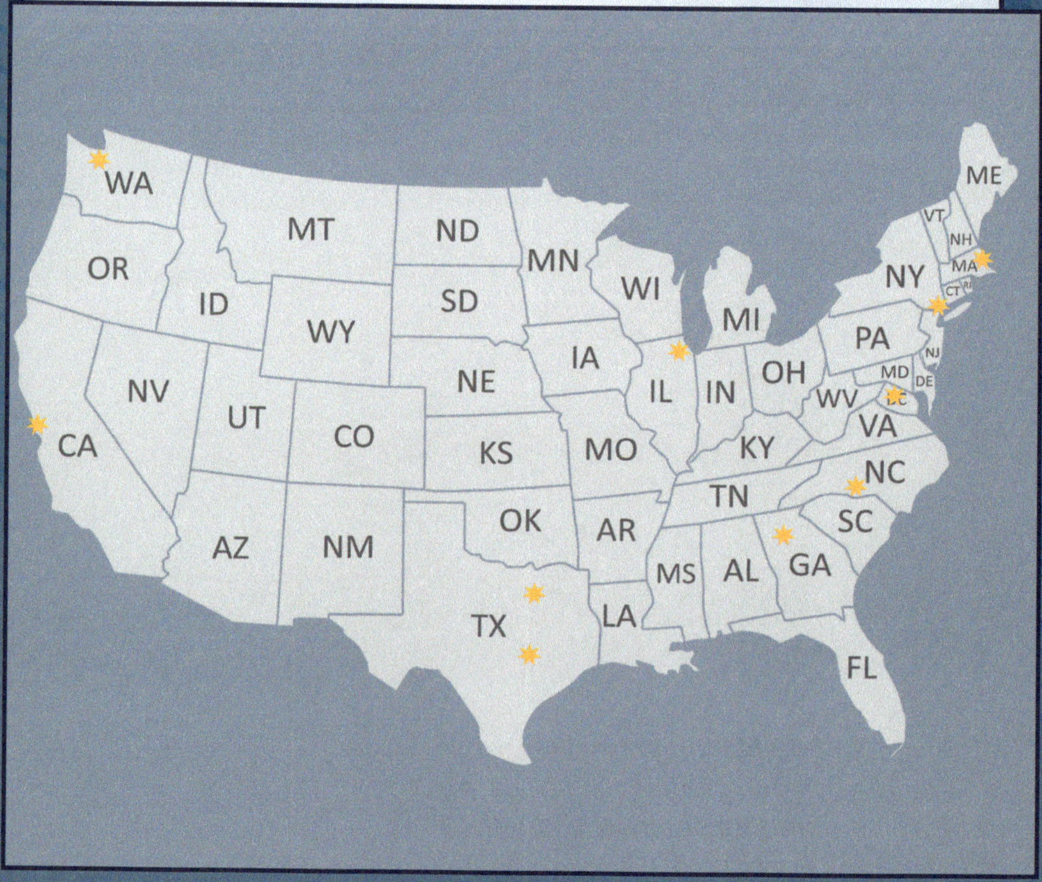

Once you have your résumé ready, it's time to create a cover letter. A cover letter accompanies your résumé and serves as a personal way to introduce yourself and your skills. All cover letters should be tailored to each job posting and should be addressed to an individual. You may need to do some research to find out who is conducting the interviews for the position. A cover letter should not list the skills you covered on your résumé, but instead should speak more personally about how you are a good fit for the position at hand. Explain how a particular experience you had makes you a good candidate, or how your particular knowledge is especially suited for the position. The cover letter is an opportunity to expand on one or two important points of your résumé and why those points make you an especially strong candidate for the position.

If your cover letter and résumé make it past the hiring manager's desk and you're invited to an interview, you'll need to prepare. Interviews can be stressful yet exciting opportunities.

Most Common Interviewing Questions

Interviews are a chance for an organization to get to know you and your skill set, ask about your previous experience, and learn about your career goals and aspirations. Here's a rundown of common interview questions and how to answer them effectively.

Tell me about yourself. This question is not about your life story, so pass up the opportunity to tell the interviewer where you grew up or that you were president of the French club in high school. Instead, share facts about your relevant education, your internship or co-op experiences, and your career goals.

Where do you see yourself in five years? Ten years? The interviewer wants to know what your career aspirations are. Do you have your sights set on becoming a leader? Do you want to manage people or projects? Companies like to hire people who are ambitious.

Tell me what you know about this company. When you interview for an organization, they want to know you've done your homework and you know who they are and what they do. Before your interview spend some time reading up on the company. What products do they make? What are their services? Who are their customers? Not only does this show that you are interested in what they do, but it also shows you can more directly relate your experiences to specific issues or trends the company is experiencing.

Tell me about a time you made a mistake. Despite the presumably negative nature of this question, the interviewer is not searching for a reason not to hire you. He or she wants to know how you learned from your

An interview is your opportunity to talk about what you can do for a company. Be prepared by thinking through answers to common questions and have a list of questions ready.

mistakes and what you did when you faced a challenge at work. Remain positive in your response and be humble about what you learned from the mistake.

What motivates you? Hiring managers want to know why you feel compelled to do a good job. Avoid mentioning money or benefits like extended vacation time. Focus your answer on positives like recognition for a job well done, personal rewards such as becoming a leader in your field, or making a meaningful contribution to the company.

What are your weaknesses? As people interview for a job, they will always talk about strengths and what they can offer a company. But hiring managers want to know what your weaknesses are, too. Choose to talk about weaknesses that you can turn into positives. Being a perfectionist means you're committed to your job. Don't admit to your habit of showing up late to work or always needing to leave early.

Do you have any questions to ask me? With this question, interviewers want to know what you are interested in learning about the company. While a hiring manager is trying to decide if you're a good fit, you need to learn about whether the company is some place where you can be happy, perform fulfilling work, and continue to grow professionally. You'll also want to know about the culture of a company. Is this an organization that shares your values and is compatible with your work style? This is an opportunity for you to learn if this is an organization where you can thrive professionally.

Staying on Top of Your Game: Professional Development

Professional development is continued learning that happens after you get a job. It can include additional courses at the college level, or seminars and conferences where you learn what's new in your field. Computing is a particularly fast-moving field where advances and new technology are emerging all the time. It's important to stay on top of new trends to learn how you can adapt them to your job.

Professional development opportunities can come from taking additional college-level courses in a particular area of computing that you want to learn more about, from attending an industry conference where computing professionals gather to share their insight and knowledge of new trends, or from course work offered by your own company. Many companies bring in leading professionals or experts to speak on a particular topic.

Professional development is an investment in your career, and companies know that if they promote your interests in learning you'll be more engaged at work and more productive. Plus, it gives a company a chance to further your skills, which enables you to grow.

GLOSSARY

ANALYTICS The method of looking at information through logical analysis.

ARCHITECTURE The method and organization of a computer or computer system.

ARTIFICIAL INTELLIGENCE An area of computing in which machines have the ability to respond in a way that suggests human intelligence.

CONSUMER A person who buys products.

CYBER A term used to classify something as related to computers and computer networks.

DATABASE A collection of information that is organized and stored on a computer.

DATA MINING The act of searching for information in a database.

EXPERIENTIAL An experience or observation that provides knowledge.

HARDWARE The physical assets of a computer system, such as a screen or a hard drive.

HUMAN-COMPUTER INTERACTION The interface between computers and computing systems and the people who use them.

INFRASTRUCTURE The organizational structure of a computer system.

INITIATIVE The ability to take action independently before others do.

NOT-FOR-PROFIT An organization that does not profit from its revenue.

SERVER A main computer system that provides files and services to other computer systems.

SOFTWARE The programs and other operating information that are run on a computer system.

SUPERVISOR A person who is in charge of others and their actions.

SUSTAINABLE Resources that are used without harming the environment.

TRIGONOMETRY An area of math that relates to the sides and angles of triangles.

USABILITY The ability for a computer system to be used efficiently by a user.

VELOCITY The speed of information.

ACTUA

15 York Street (Courtyard)
Ottawa, ON K1N 5S7
Canada
(613) 234 4137
Website: http://actua.ca
ACTUA is a national charity that prepares Canadian youth to become innovators and leaders by engaging them in exciting STEM experiences that build critical skills and confidence. The organization is a strong advocate for engaging kids in STEM.

Association of Information Technology Professionals

1120 Route 73, Suite 200
Mount Laurel, NJ 08054-5113
(800) 224-9371
Website: https://www.aitp.org
The Association of Information Technology Professionals works to advance the IT profession through professional development, the support and advocacy of IT education, and through the creation of national policy to help direct and guide the IT profession.

Association for Women in Computing

PO Box 2768
Oakland, CA 94602
Info@awc-hq.org
Website: http://www.awc-hq.org/home.html

The Association for Women in Computing is one of the first professional organizations created to promote the advancement of women in computing professions. The organization has a professional membership, as well as student chapters at colleges and universities to encourage young women to pursue careers in the computing industry.

Code.org

1501 4th Avenue, Suite 900
Seattle, WA 98101
Website: https://code.org
Code.org is dedicated to expanding access to computer science. Their goals are to increase the participation of women and underrepresented students of color and to provide students in all schools with an opportunity to learn about computer science.

Girls Who Code

https://girlswhocode.com/
Girlswhocode.org is the largest computer science program for girls in the nation. They are dedicated to closing the gender gap in the technology and computing fields by creating opportunities for your girls to learn about and participate in activities designed to increase these students' potential for success in a computing and tech career.

IRIDESCENT

13701 Marina Pointe
Marina Del Rey, CA 90292
(877) 829-5500
Website: http://iridescentlearning.org
Iridescent is an educational organization that provides training and guidance to professional engineers and scientists to become mentors. These mentors help to provide STEM (science, technology, engineering, and math) education to underserved girls and children.

Kids Code Jeunesse

51 Sherbrooke Ouest
Montréal, QC H2X 1X2
Canada
contact@kidscodejeunesse.org
Website: http://kidscodejeunesse.org/home
Kids Code Jeunesse is a Canadian not for profit organization that empowers kids, teachers, and parents to thrive in a technology driven society. The organization provides educational materials for teachers and hosts workshops for kids and parents for those who want to learn to code.

National Center for Women in Technology

1111 Engineering Drive, ECCE 1B-36
Boulder, CO 80309
(303) 735-6671
Website: https://www.ncwit.org
Founded in 2004 by the National Science Foundation, the National Center for Women in Technology strives to increase the participation of girls and women in computing.

Websites

Because of the changing nature of internet links, Rosen Publishing has developed an online list of websites related to the subject of this book. This site is updated regularly. Please use this link to access the list:

http://www.rosenlinks.com/TECHT/data

For Further Reading

Bedell, Jane. *So, You Want to Be a Coder?: The Ultimate Guide to Programming, Video Game Creation, Robotics, and More.* Hillsboro, OR: Aladdin/Beyond Words Publishing, 2016.

Bonnice, Sherry. *Careers with Character: Computer Programmer.* Broomall, PA: Mason Crest Publishers, 2013.

Briggs, Jason R. *Python for Kids: A Playful Introduction to Programming.* San Francisco, CA: No Starch Press, 2010.

Croce, Nicholas. *Enhancing Your Academic Digital Footprint.* New York, NY: Rosen Publishing Group, 2012.

Eboch, MM. *Big Data and Privacy Rights.* Edina, MN: Essential Library/ABDO Publishing, 2016.

Grayson, Robert. *Managing Your Digital Footprint.* New York, NY: Rosen Publishing Group, 2012.

Mozer, Mindy. *Big Data and You.* New York, NY: Rosen Publishing Group, 2014.

Reynolds, Vince. *Big Data for Beginners.* San Francisco, CA: Amazon Creative Services, 2016

Sande, Warren, and Carter Sande. *Hello World! Computer Programming for Kids and Other Beginners.* Shelter Island, NY: Manning Publications, 2009.

Swanson, Jennifer, and Glen Mullaly. *How The Internet Works.* North Mankato, MN: Child's World Publishing, 2011.

BIBLIOGRAPHY

"Best Global Universities for Computer Science." USNews.com. Retrieved September 28, 2016. http://www.usnews.com/education/best-global-universities/computer-science.

Bischof, Hans-Peter. "Computer Science, MS." RIT.edu. Retrieved September 30, 2016. https://www.rit.edu/programs/computer-science-ms.

"Degree Requirements: Software Engineering." Drexel.edu. September 2016. http://catalog.drexel.edu/undergraduate/collegeofcomputingandinformatics/softwareengineering/#degreerequirementstext.

"50 Most Common Interview Questions." Glassdoor.com. March 25, 2016. https://www.glassdoor.com/blog/common-interview-questions/.

"How to Write a Resume: Resume Tips." Monster.com. Retrieved September 30, 2016. http://www.monster.com/career-advice/article/how-to-write-a-resume.

Kolakowski, Nick. "Top Cities for the Autumn Job Hunt." Dice.com. October 17, 2016. http://insights.dice.com/2016/10/17/top-cities-autumn-job-hunt/.

Landau, Elizabeth. "Google Tool Uses Search Terms to Detect Flu Outbreaks." CNN.com. December 9, 2008. http://www.cnn.com/2008/HEALTH/conditions/11/11/google.flu.trends/.

Lipman, Victor. "Why Employee Development Is Important." Forbes.com. January 29, 2013. http://www.forbes.com/sites/victorlipman/2013/01/29

/why-development-planning-is-important-neglected-and-can-cost-you-young-talent/#6349ec6a2ce0.
Manyika, James, Michael Chui, Brad Brown, Jacques Bughin, Richard Dobbs, Charles Roxburgh, Angela Hung Byers. "Big Data: The Next Frontier for Innovation, Competition and Productivity." Mckinsey.com. Retrieved September 28, 2016. http://www.mckinsey.com/business-functions/business-technology/our-insights/big-data-the-next-frontier-for-innovation.
Matsudaira, Kate. "The Skills Needed by Big Data Engineers." Dice.com. August 21, 2014. http://insights.dice.com/2014/08/21/key-skills-needed-big-data-engineers/.
McKendrick, Joe. "7 New Types of Jobs Created by Dig Data." ZDNet.com. September 20, 2012. http://www.zdnet.com/article/7-new-types-of-jobs-created-by-big-data/.
McKendrick, Joe. "12 Business Skills That Will Never, Ever Go out of Style." ZDNet.com. March 11, 2013. http://www.zdnet.com/article/12-business-skills-that-will-never-ever-go-out-of-style/.
McNulty, Eileen. "Understanding Big Data Infrastructure." Dataconomy.com. June 19, 2014. http://dataconomy.com/understanding-big-data-infrastructure/.
Nemschoff, Michele. "7 Important Types of Big Data." Smartdatacollective.com. February 26, 2014. http://www.smartdatacollective.com/michelenemschoff/187751/7-important-types-big-data.

"PLTW Computer Science (9-12)." PLTW.org. Retrieved September 28, 2016. https://www.pltw.org/our-programs/pltw-computer-science.

Shaw, Jonathan. "Why 'Big Data' Is a Big Deal." Harvard-magazine.com. April 2014. http://harvardmagazine.com/2014/03/why-big-data-is-a-big-deal.

Tobak, Steve. "5 Skills You Must Develop to Succeed in Business." Entrepreneur.com. November 12, 2015. https://www.entrepreneur.com/article/250851.

Weaver, Matthew. "Google Hits to Warn of Flu Epidemic." Theguardian.com. November 12, 2008. https://www.theguardian.com/technology/2008/nov/12/google-health.

INDEX

S

T

U

V

X

Y

ABOUT THE AUTHOR

Laura La Bella has written several nonfiction children's books. She works full time at Rochester Institute of Technology as a marketing communications writer, editor, and web content manager. She lives in Rochester, New York, with her husband and two sons.

PHOTO CREDITS:

Cover, p. 1 ESB Professional/Shutterstock.com; pp. 4-5 3DSculptor/iStock/Thinkstock; pp. 6-7 laflor/E+/Getty Images; p. 8 shironosov/iStock/Thinkstock; p. 10 gpointstudio/iStock/Thinkstock; p. 11 OmaPhoto/iStock/Thinkstock; p. 13 blackzheep/Shutterstock.com; p. 15 bodym/iStock/Thinkstock; p. 17 Rubberball/Mike Kemp/Getty Images; p. 21 Chesky_W/iStock/Thinkstock; p. 23 PeopleImages/E+/Getty Images; p. 30 Pressmaster/Shutterstock.com; p. 33 Fuse/Corbis/Getty Images; pp. 35, 63 asiseeit/E+/Getty Images; p. 37 Dieter Scheqig/Westend61/Getty Images; p. 42 Hero Images/Getty Images; p. 45 Peter Dazeley/The Image Bank/Getty Images; p. 46 vgajic/E+/Getty Images; p. 48 KatarzynaBialasiewicz/iStock/Thinkstock; p. 52 Tom Merton/Caiaimage/Getty Images; pp. 56-57 Reuters/Alamy Stock Photo; p. 58 © iStockphoto.com/milindri; p. 59 Andrey_Popov/Shutterstock.com; p. 60 Luchenko Yana/Shutterstock.com; cover and interior pages background designs mydegage/Shutterstock.com, Digital_Art/Shutterstock.com, DrHitch/Shutterstock.com.

Series Designer/Book Layout: Brian Garvey; Editor: Carolyn DeCarlo; Photo Researcher: Karen Huang